VIETNAM

The Story of a Marine

Dee Phillips

Yesterday's Voices

Images courtesy of Alamy (pages 16–17c), AP/Press Association Images (page 24), Corbis (pages 1, 13t, 15t, 26t, 28, 30, 38–39, 43, 44b), Getty Images (page 23), and Shutterstock.

Acknowledgements: With thanks to Lorraine Petersen, Educational Consultant, for her help in the development and creation of these books.

SADDLEBACK
EDUCATIONAL PUBLISHING
www.sdlback.com

ISBN-13: 978-1-62250-911-9
ISBN-10: 1-62250-911-0
eBook: 978-1-63078-037-1

Printed in Malaysia

20 19 18 17 16   2 3 4 5 6

Every day we went on patrol.
The Vietcong were everywhere.
Hiding in the jungles. Hiding in villages.
We had to find them … before they found us.

VIETNAM
The Story of a Marine

In the 1960s, South Vietnam was at war.

Their enemies were North Vietnam and an army of rebels from the south called the Vietcong.

The United States supported the government of South Vietnam.

American troops were sent to Vietnam to fight.

Some young Americans enlisted. They knew they might go to Vietnam.

Others did not have a choice.

They were made to join the armed forces by the U.S. government. This was known as the draft.

Many Americans did not want their country to fight in this faraway war.

I look into her eyes.
She looks into mine.
She's just a kid. Maybe 15 or 16.
Her rifle is just inches from my face.

She screams at me.
I don't know what she's saying.
I only know one thing.

I don't want to die in Vietnam.

I look into the girl's eyes.
She jabs her rifle at my face.

No more than a second passes,
but time stands still.
I hear Eddie's voice.

*"You won't be around to hear
Mom's screams."*

Eddie. My brother. My twin.
Mom always said she could
feel us fighting inside her.

We came into the world on
the same day.

That was the last time we ever
agreed on anything.

I couldn't wait for high
school to be over.
All I ever wanted was to
be a marine.
There was a war going on,
and I wanted in!

I signed up as soon as I was 18.

All Eddie ever wanted was
to be a doctor.

Eddie didn't agree with killing.

He didn't think Americans should
fight in someone else's war.

"Don't you see the bodies on
the news?" he shouted.

"You won't be here when they
knock on the door. You won't be
around to hear Mom's screams."

NOT OUR SONS
NOT YOUR SONS
NOT THEIR SONS

I couldn't wait to get to boot camp.
I got off the bus feeling like a man.

By the end of my first day, I was a scared kid.

A scared kid with a shaved head.

RUNNING

POLISHING

SHOOTING

MARCHING

PUSH-UPS

SIT-UPS

SCRUBBING

If one guy screwed up, we all got punished.

I wished Eddie was there with me.

That scared kid turned into a marine.

I went home on leave.
Mom cried when she saw me in
my uniform.
But Eddie couldn't look me in the eye.

"I can't believe you're going to fight this
war!" he shouted.

"Well, I'm proud to fight for my country,"
I shouted back. "You're just a coward!"

It was the worst fight we ever had.

The girl soldier jabs her rifle at my face.
She screams at me.
I don't know what she's saying.
I only know one thing.
I'm going to have to shoot this girl.

It's her or me.

I couldn't wait to get to Vietnam.
Every day we went on patrol.

There were no battlefields in this war.
The Vietcong were everywhere.
Hiding in the jungles.
Hiding in villages.

We had to find them ...
before they found us.

You think you know what fear is.
But you don't.

We were on patrol in rice fields.
We came under fire.
I crawled through the water on my belly.
Bullets hit the ground all around me.

Our choppers flew in.
They blew the enemy apart and
rescued us.

That was a good day.

You think you can imagine
what death looks like.
But you can't.

We were on patrol in a jungle.

BANG!

One of our guys touched a trip wire.
The land mine blew him apart.

I found his dog tags hanging from a tree.

I missed my brother.

Every time I hung out with the guys,
I thought of Eddie.
Every time I heard a joke,
I wanted to tell him.

I thought about the fight.
We'd make up when I got home.

The months passed by.

Some days were boring.
Some days were terrifying.
But I loved being a marine.

I was proud to fight for my country.

But it was tough.
I lost so many friends.

Then came that night.
We were searching a village.
There were Vietcong
hiding there.
I crept into a hut.
That's where I found the girl.

She jabs her rifle at my face.
She screams at me.
I'm going to have to shoot
this girl.
It's her or me.

BANG!

I wake up with a jolt.
I lie in the darkness.

I didn't die that night,
but I relive it in my dreams.

Again and again for nearly 50 years.

Somehow I survived that night.
A Vietcong shell hit the hut.
It blew the young girl apart.
I crawled from the hut, burned but alive.

Somehow I survived the war.

I slowly walk along the wall.
After all these years,
I know where I'm heading.

In the end, even Eddie had to go.
He was drafted and sent to Vietnam.
Eddie. My brother. The coward.

I couldn't have been more wrong.

Eddie was killed in Vietnam.
He took a bullet to the head.

There was a little kid.
She was trapped between
our guys and the enemy.
Eddie died trying to save
that little kid.

He was right about one thing.
I wasn't around to hear Mom's screams.

I find his name on the wall.
Eddie. My brother. My twin.

We never did patch up that fight.

I gently touch the cool stone
and close my eyes.
I just hope he's out there
somewhere.

And that he knows....

VIETNAM
Behind the Story

In the 1960s, North Vietnam was a communist nation. The government controlled land, business, and property. People were not as free to make changes to their lives as people living in a democratic nation, such as the United States. South Vietnam was not communist. North Vietnam was at war with South Vietnam. The north also supported the Vietcong, an army of communist rebels in the south.

So why did the U.S. get involved in the Vietnam War? The U.S. claimed that if South Vietnam fell, it would lead to communism spreading to other parts of the world. The U.S. became an ally, or partner, of South Vietnam.

Many Americans opposed the war. They did not believe that fighting in Vietnam protected democracy. They did not trust the South Vietnamese government. A large anti-war movement began.

In 1973, the U.S. withdrew from Vietnam. In 1975, North Vietnam took over all of Vietnam. Many Americans felt the war was a terrible waste of lives. More than 58,000 Americans died in Vietnam. It's estimated that more than three million Vietnamese soldiers and civilians were killed.

The Draft

During the 1960s and 1970s, young American men had to be available to serve in the military. When the U.S. entered the Vietnam War, many of them were called up, or drafted. They had to join the U.S. armed forces, even if they didn't agree with the war and didn't want to fight.

Thousands of Americans protested against the war at meetings and marches.

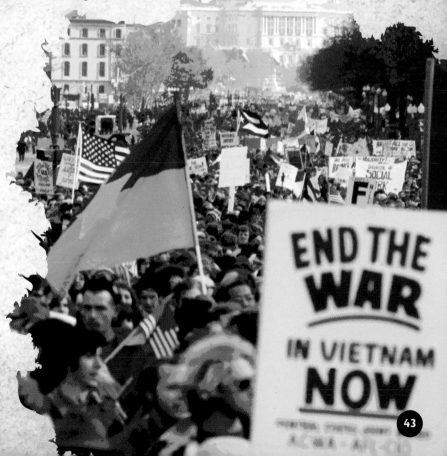

END THE WAR IN VIETNAM NOW

VIETNAM
What's next?

At the end of the story, the main character thinks about his brother, Eddie. He has lots of feelings that he would like Eddie to know about. Look back through the story.

What clues to the brothers' relationship and feelings can you find?

What things do you think the marine would like to tell Eddie if he could?

During wars, photographers and filmmakers often put themselves in danger to record what is happening. Many photos from the Vietnam War are famous because they had a powerful effect on people back home.

The photos in this book that show soldiers in Vietnam are real photos from the war. Which one do you think is the most powerful? How does the photo make you feel?

Many songs were written about the Vietnam War. You can find them and listen to them online. Try writing your own song about the war. You can use the story of the twin brothers as your inspiration or think of a different idea for the theme of your Vietnam War song.

The twin brothers are characters in a story. The things they experienced in Vietnam happened to thousands of young men, though. At the end of the book, the marine visits the Vietnam Veterans Memorial (popularly known as "The Wall") in Washington, D.C.

Find out more about the memorial, the war, and the ways in which the people who died in Vietnam are remembered by visiting *http://www.vvmf.org/*

Titles in the

Yesterday's Voices

series

VIKING
The Story of a Raider
Dee Phillips

SAMURAI
The Story of a Warrior
Dee Phillips

PIRATE
The Story of a Buccaneer
Dee Phillips

We jump from our ship and attack. But something feels wrong. I know this place.

We face each other. Two proud samurai. Revenge burns in my heart.

We saw a treasure ship. Up went our black flag. They could not escape.

A DREAM OF AMERICA
The Story of an Immigrant
Dee Phillips

RESISTANCE FIGHTER
The Story of a Secret War
Dee Phillips

VIETNAM
The Story of a Marine
Dee Phillips

My body aches from the hard work. I miss my home. Will my dream of America come true?

I jumped from the plane. I carried fake papers, a gun and a radio. Now I was Sylvie, a resistance fighter.

Every day we went on patrol. The Vietcong hid in jungles and villages. We had to find them … before they found us.

GLADIATOR
The Story of a Fighter

I waited deep below the arena. Then it was my turn to fight. Kill or be killed!

RUNAWAY
The Story of a Slave

I cannot live as a slave any longer. Tonight, I will escape and never go back.

TITANIC
The Story of a Disaster

The ship is sinking into the icy sea. I don't want to die. Someone help us!

OVER THE TOP
The Story of a Soldier

I'm waiting in the trench. I am so afraid. Tomorrow we go over the top.

TAIL GUNNER
The Story of a Bombing Raid

Another night. Another bombing raid. Will this night be the one when we don't make it back?

HOLOCAUST
The Story of a Survivor

They took my clothes and shaved my head. I was no longer a human.